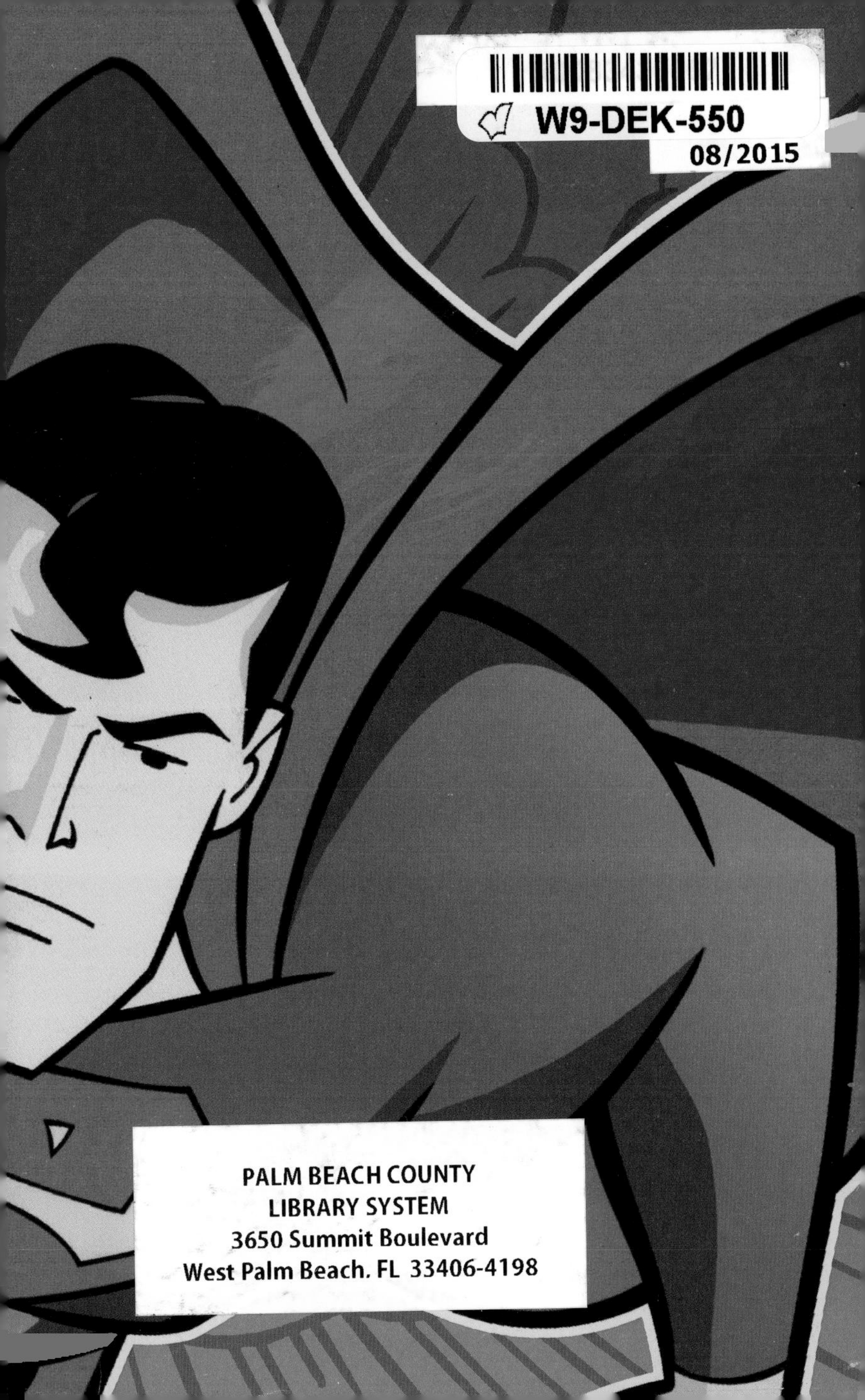

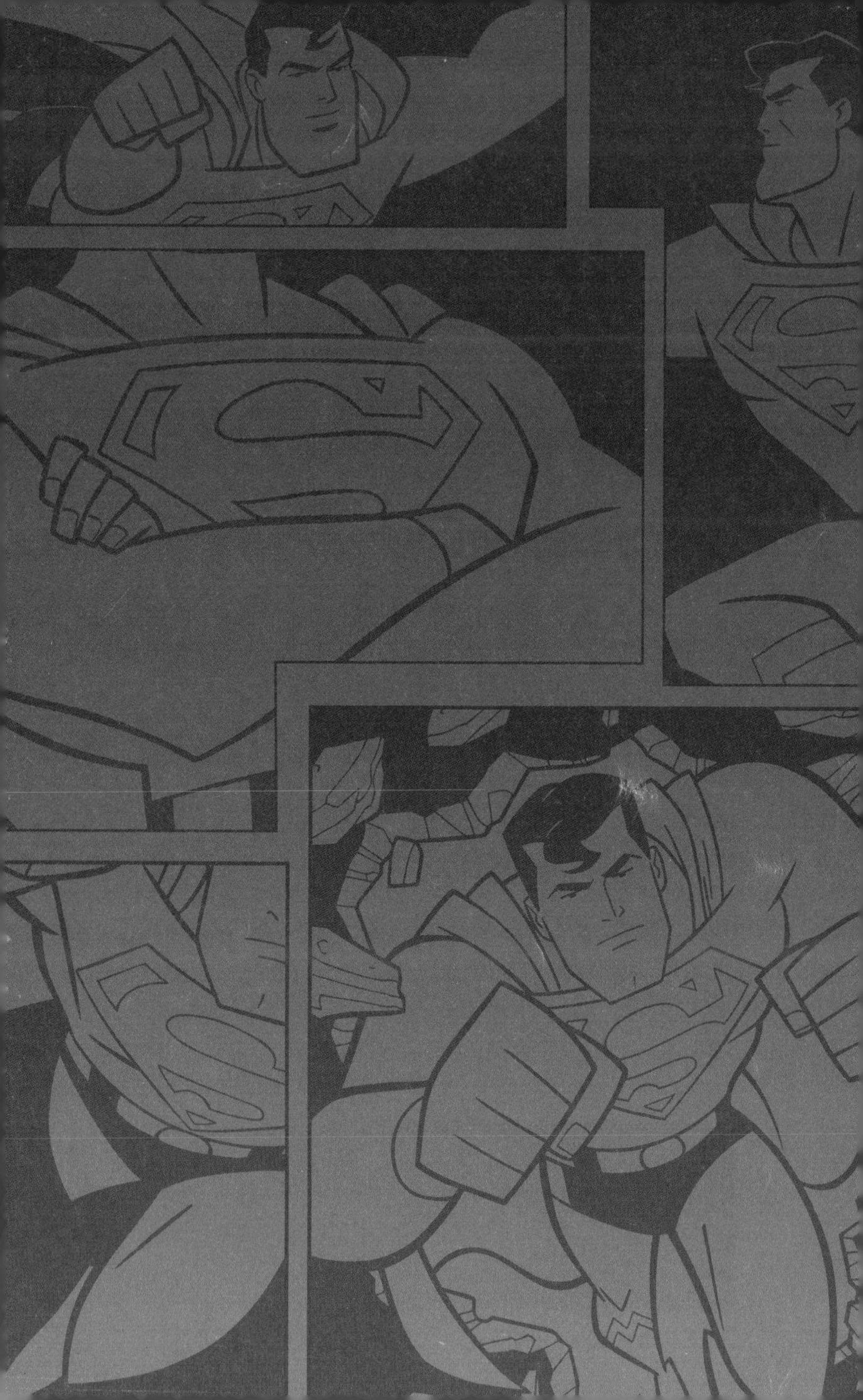

DC
COMICS™
SUPER
HEROES

SUPERMAN

LITTLE GREEN MEN

WRITTEN BY
MATTHEW K. MANNING

ILLUSTRATED BY
ERIK DOESCHER,
MIKE DeCARLO, AND
LEE LOUGHRIDGE

SUPERMAN CREATED BY
JERRY SIEGEL AND
JOE SHUSTER
BY SPECIAL ARRANGEMENT WITH
THE JERRY SIEGEL FAMILY

STONE ARCH BOOKS
a capstone imprint

Published by Stone Arch Books
A Capstone Imprint
1710 Roe Crest Drive
North Mankato, Minnesota 56003
www.capstonepub.com

Library of Congress Cataloging-in-Publication Data

Manning, Matthew K.
 Little green men / by Matthew K. Manning ; illustrated by Erik Doescher ;
illustrated by Mike DeCarlo ; illustrated by Lee Loughridge.
   p. cm. -- (DC super heroes. Superman)
 ISBN 978-1-4342-1881-0 (library binding) -- ISBN 978-1-4342-2259-6 (pbk.)
 [1. Superheroes--Fiction.] I. Doescher, Erik, ill. II. De Carlo, Mike, ill. III.
Loughridge, Lee, ill. IV. Title.
 PZ7.M315614Li 2010
 [Fic]--dc22   2009029104

Summary: Taking a rare day off from the *Daily Planet* newspaper, Clark Kent
relaxes with his new sci-fi novel, Little Green Men. Suddenly, the mild-mannered
reporter hears a scream! Unable to ignore his other job as Superman, the world's
greatest hero, he soars toward the cry for help, rescuing a construction worker from
a near fatal fall. The interruptions, however, don't stop there, and the Man of Steel's
lazy day quickly becomes stranger than fiction.

Art Director: Bob Lentz
Designer: Hilary Wacholz
Production Specialist: Michelle Biedscheid

Printed in the United States of America in North Mankato, Minnesota.
062014   008284R

TABLE OF CONTENTS

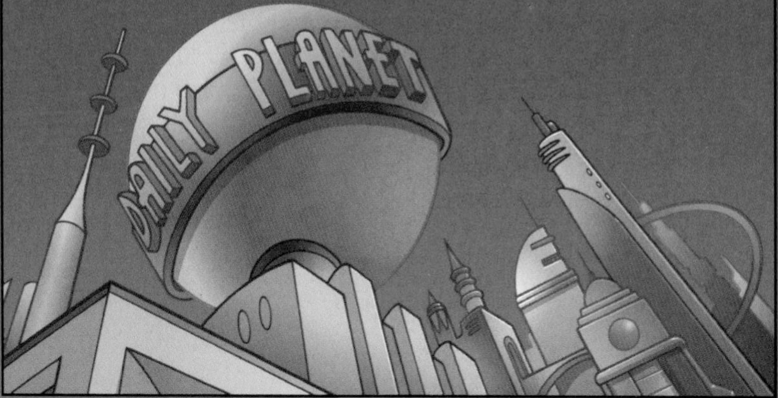

DAILY PLANET

CHAPTER 1

READER'S BLOCK

The little girl ran as fast as she could. Through all the smoke and chaos, she could still see her mother in the crowd a few yards in front of her. Try as she might, she couldn't catch up to her mother. Her legs just weren't long enough, but the little girl kept running. After all, she knew what would happen to her if she didn't.

Slowly, a shadow drifted over the little girl's head. It darkened the entire city street. The little girl stopped. She knew there was no use trying to escape.

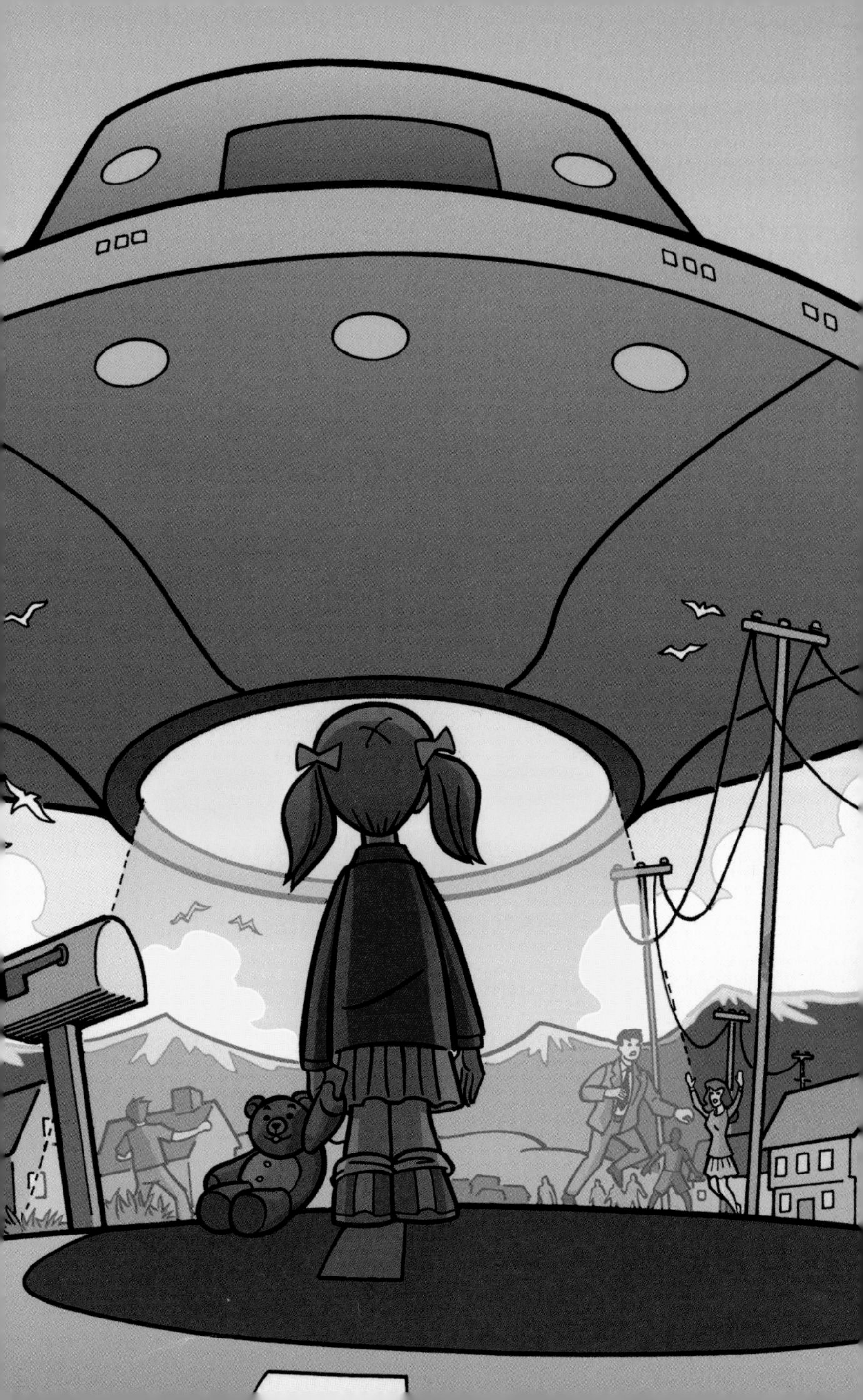

She looked up at the giant disc blocking out the sun. It wasn't what she'd expected a flying saucer to look like. They looked so much smaller in movies and on TV.

As everyone around her continued to panic and sprint through the street, the little girl stayed put and watched. She saw two tiny figures in the saucer's cockpit. The creatures had large green heads, beady eyes, and skinny bodies. She watched as one of the aliens pulled some sort of lever that hung by his head. Suddenly, the saucer began to glow a bright green color. The little girl could feel the tiny hairs on her arms stand straight up. The air seemed alive with electricity. She knew what was about to happen. She had seen it on TV. Any minute now they would —

CLINK CLINK CLANK!

Clark Kent jumped at the loud noise. It came from outside his window. The pounding made it impossible to read.

He set down his copy of *Little Green Men* on his coffee table. As he walked across his living room, he saw what was causing all the commotion. A construction worker was using a jackhammer on the sidewalk on the other side of the street.

For several weeks now, workers had been building a new high-rise apartment complex on his street. Right now, the building was just steel beams and concrete. People in orange hard hats were working on every single floor of the structure.

Clark shut his window. He knew the men were just doing their jobs. But did they have to do it so loudly?

It was Clark's one day off. He wouldn't be working on any new articles as a reporter for the *Daily Planet* today. And he wouldn't be off fighting crime and saving the world as his secret identity, Superman. No, for one Saturday afternoon, Clark Kent was going to relax. After all, he'd just received a new science fiction novel in the mail today. It was written by his favorite author, Kurt Vandelay.

Getting comfortable in his chair again, Clark picked up his book. He looked at the cover. It was a picture of a flying saucer with two tiny aliens onboard. The text read "*Little Green Men* by Kurt Vandelay." Clark couldn't help but smile. He always found it funny to see how humans pictured aliens. After all, Clark Kent himself was from another planet.

Although he kept it a secret, Clark's real name was Kal-El. He was born on a planet called Krypton. He was sent to Earth in a rocket when his home had been destroyed in a giant explosion. When he crash-landed in a field in Kansas, he was just a baby, appearing as human as anyone else. As he got older, he discovered that Earth's yellow sun gave him strange powers. He could fly. He could run faster than a speeding bullet. He was stronger than the most powerful freight train. When he grew up, Clark adopted the identity of Superman. Then he set out to protect his new home planet.

The red cape was hung up for the afternoon. Instead, Clark leaned back in his chair. Turning the first page of his book, he did his best to block out the noise from outside.

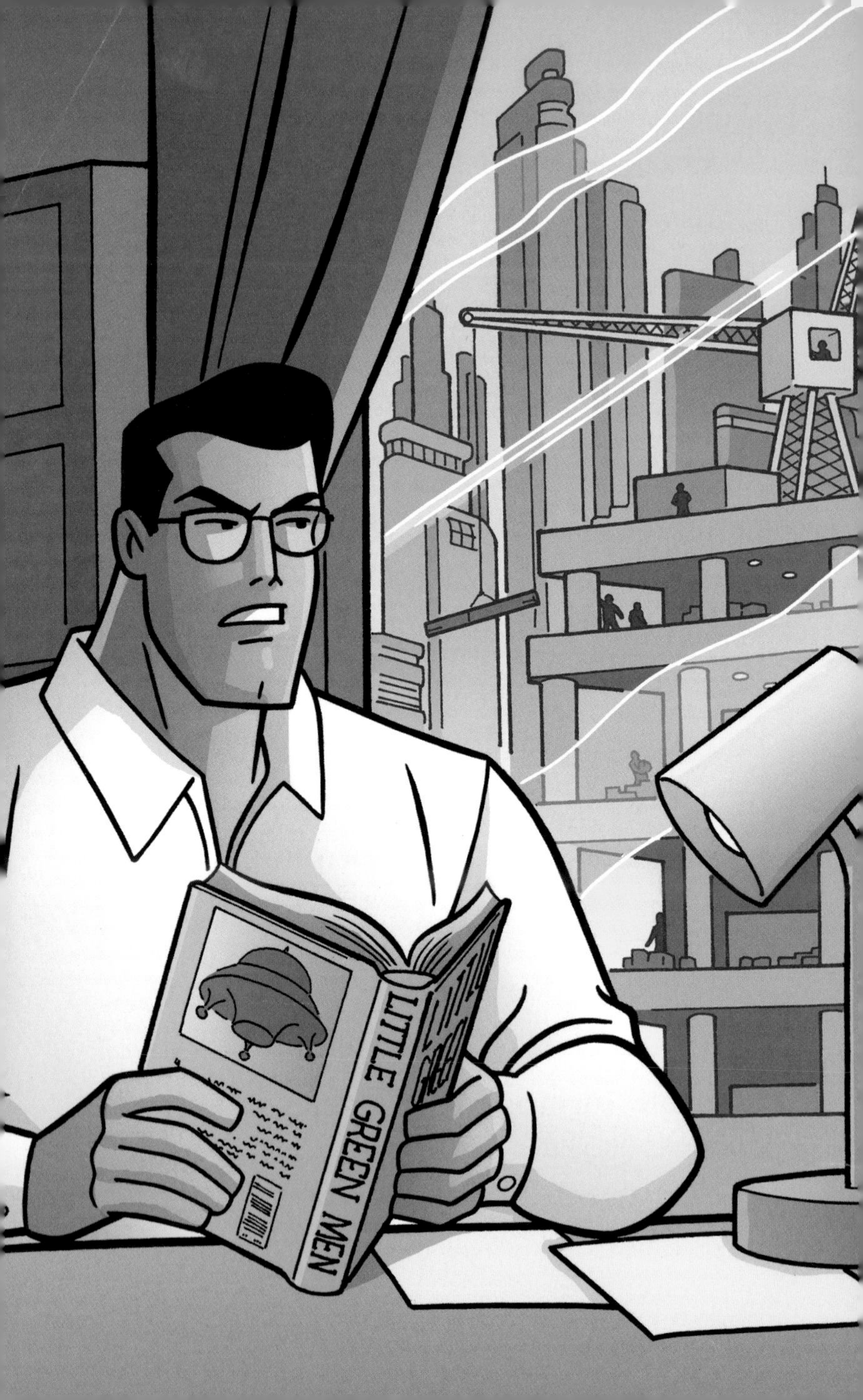
LITTLE GREEN MEN

CLANK! CLANK! CLANK!

It was no use. Even with the window closed, Clark couldn't block out the sound of that jackhammer. That was one problem with being a Kryptonian. Along with his other senses, Clark's hearing was also magnified. If he listened closely, he could hear a whisper from miles away. He could eavesdrop on a movie from across town. Clark could even hear a fly land on a wall in his neighbor's apartment.

Since he had possessed this power for most of his life, Clark had learned to ignore most noises. But some sounds were impossible to block out. A jackhammer was one of them.

Clark leaned his head into the palm of his hand and sighed. This just wasn't working out.

As Clark stood up in frustration, he heard something different from the construction site. It was a faint voice. He could barely detect it under all the noise from the jackhammer. He listened closely, and he heard it again. It was a cry for help!

At nearly the speed of light, Clark changed into his Superman costume. Yes, Superman could block out many sounds. A cry for help was certainly not one of them.

CHAPTER 2

CONFLICTING STORIES

Tommy Gallagher's goal in life was to work on a skyscraper. Ever since he had moved to Metropolis, Tommy had been fascinated by the city's amazing buildings. He had marveled at the men and women brave enough to work up on the high beams of the city's many construction sites.

He had always wished that someday, he too could help build something truly impressive. But today, as he fell thirty stories to what was sure to be his death, Tommy started to rethink his life goals.

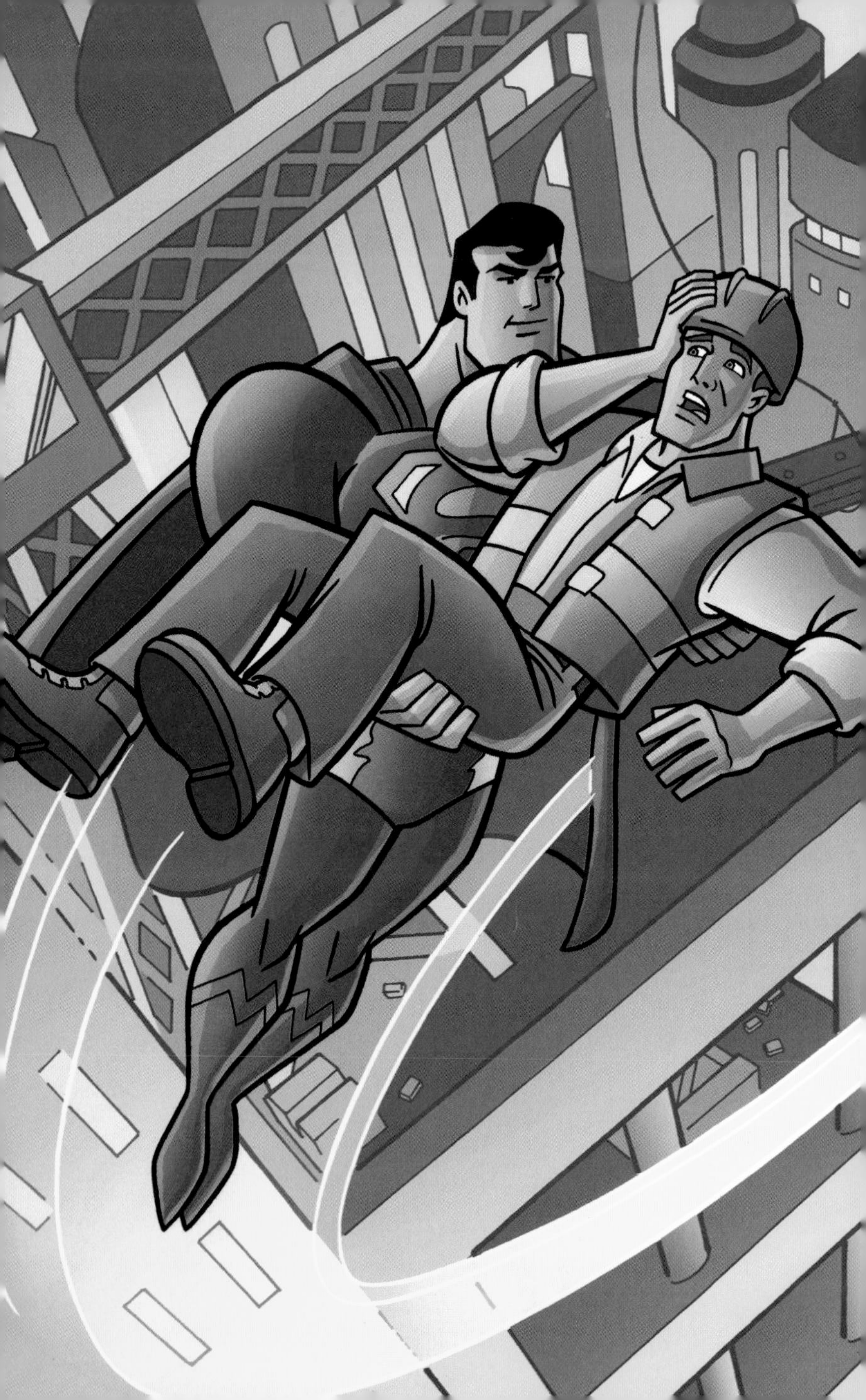

Tommy pinched his eyes shut. He braced himself for impact. All of a sudden, he realized he was no longer falling. Instead, he was being lifted higher into the air. Tommy opened his eyes. He couldn't believe it. Superman had caught him!

"There you go," Superman said. He placed Tommy back on a building high above the city streets.

"Thanks," Tommy said. He felt nervous talking to the Man of Steel.

"If you don't mind my asking," Superman said, "how did you lose your footing? You construction workers usually seem to know what you're doing."

"Oh, yeah. It was the weirdest thing, Superman," Tommy said, straightening his safety helmet.

"I was securing a beam on the 31st floor," Tommy said. " Then suddenly, this . . . *thing* just buzzed right past my head. I don't know what it was, but it almost hit me!"

Superman floated in mid-air across from Tommy for a moment. It sounded like there was more going on here than he had thought. Superman waved good-bye to Tommy and flew away. Behind him, Tommy yelled his thanks.

Superman cleared his head. He would worry more about all this later. Right now, it was time to get back to his book. He just needed to find a better place to read it.

*   *   *

A few moments and one wardrobe change later, Clark was reading again.

He was happily seated on a comfortable wooden bench in Metropolis's Centennial Park. Clark had managed to find a quiet little corner in the shade. Very few people were around.

There was no construction noise at all. In fact, the only sounds were coming from the wind rustling through the trees. Clark couldn't have asked for a more perfect setting. Smiling, he opened his book to the first chapter.

"Excuse me," said a quiet voice. "Is this seat taken?"

Clark looked up to see an elderly woman holding two knitting needles and a bag of yarn. "No," he said, pointing to the other side of his bench. "Feel free."

"Thank you, young man," said the lady.

Clark smiled at her and returned his gaze to his book.

"What are you reading?" the woman asked.

"It's the new Kurt Vandelay novel," Clarks said rather quickly. He didn't want to be rude, but he hadn't even finished reading the first page.

"I know that author," the woman said. "Kurt Vandelay, I mean. Well, I don't know him personally, but I know who he is."

"Oh?" Clark said in a monotone voice. Talking about his book was in no way as fun as actually reading it.

"Yes, he lives in the city, I believe," the woman said. "A lot of famous people live in the city."

"Huh," Clark said.

Clark was finding it hard to concentrate. He realized he had reread the same sentence a few dozen times by now.

"Oh, yes. There's that lady from the news. She lives here. You know the one," the old woman said, pointing her sewing needles in the air. "The one with the pretty smile and the makeup. And there's that handsome fellow from the motion pictures," the woman continued. "Christopher something, I think. He's quite handsome."

Clark stayed silent. He just politely smiled, hoping that the conversation would end soon.

"Yes, he lives downtown, I think," the woman continued. "I saw a program about his home. It's quite large. He has a very nice kitchen. All new appliances."

"I'm sorry —" Clark started to say. But he suddenly stopped himself. His super-hearing had detected something from across town. It sounded like an explosion. He could hear yelling, and the crackling of spreading flames.

"Excuse me," Clark said, standing up. "I need to get going."

The woman looked back at her yarn and rolled her eyes. "Well," she said in a huff. "I guess some people are just too busy for a little friendly conversation these days."

Suddenly, a gust of wind knocked the yarn out of her hands. Clark Kent was nowhere to be seen.

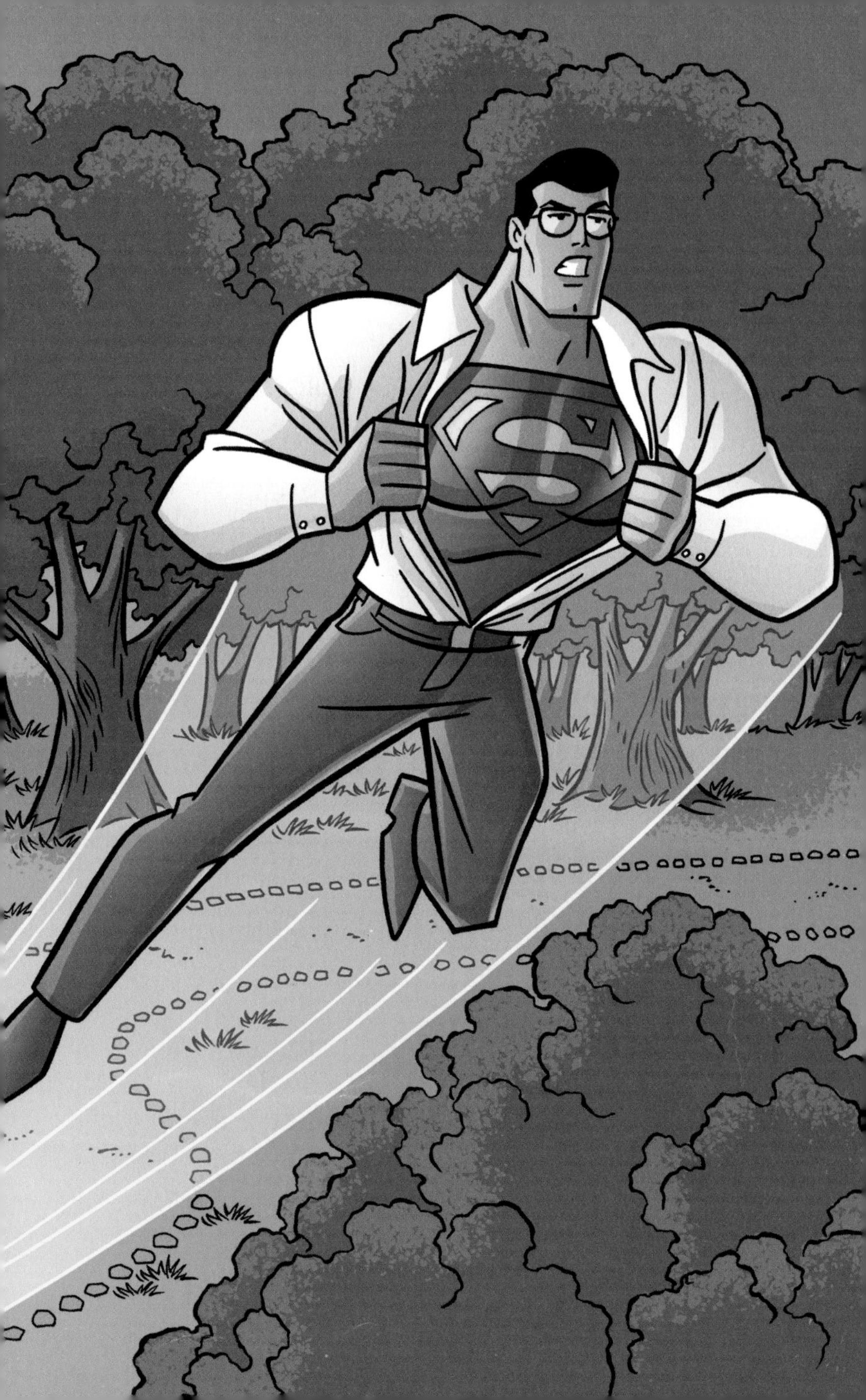

CHAPTER 3

STRANGER THAN FICTION

The fire was raging by the time Superman arrived. He recognized the building. It was a branch of S.T.A.R. Labs, a wing dedicated to the advancement and research of aerospace technology. They developed everything from experimental rocket fuel to jet engines. Since their projects were usually very large, the building was one of the biggest factories in Metropolis.

BZZT! Superman surveyed the building with his X-ray vision.

It seemed that all of the rooms were empty. The fire had spread across the entire building, but all the employees had managed to exit safely. However, the flames seemed to be spreading. It wouldn't be long before one of the neighboring buildings caught fire.

Superman knew what he had to do. Rising into the air in front of the building, he took in a deep breath. Concentrating on the fire, Superman opened his mouth slightly. Then, he blew all the air out of his lungs through the small opening in his mouth.

WHOOOOSH!

Whenever air is forced through a small hole at an incredible speed, it cools very fast. In Superman's case, this causes what some people have called his freeze breath.

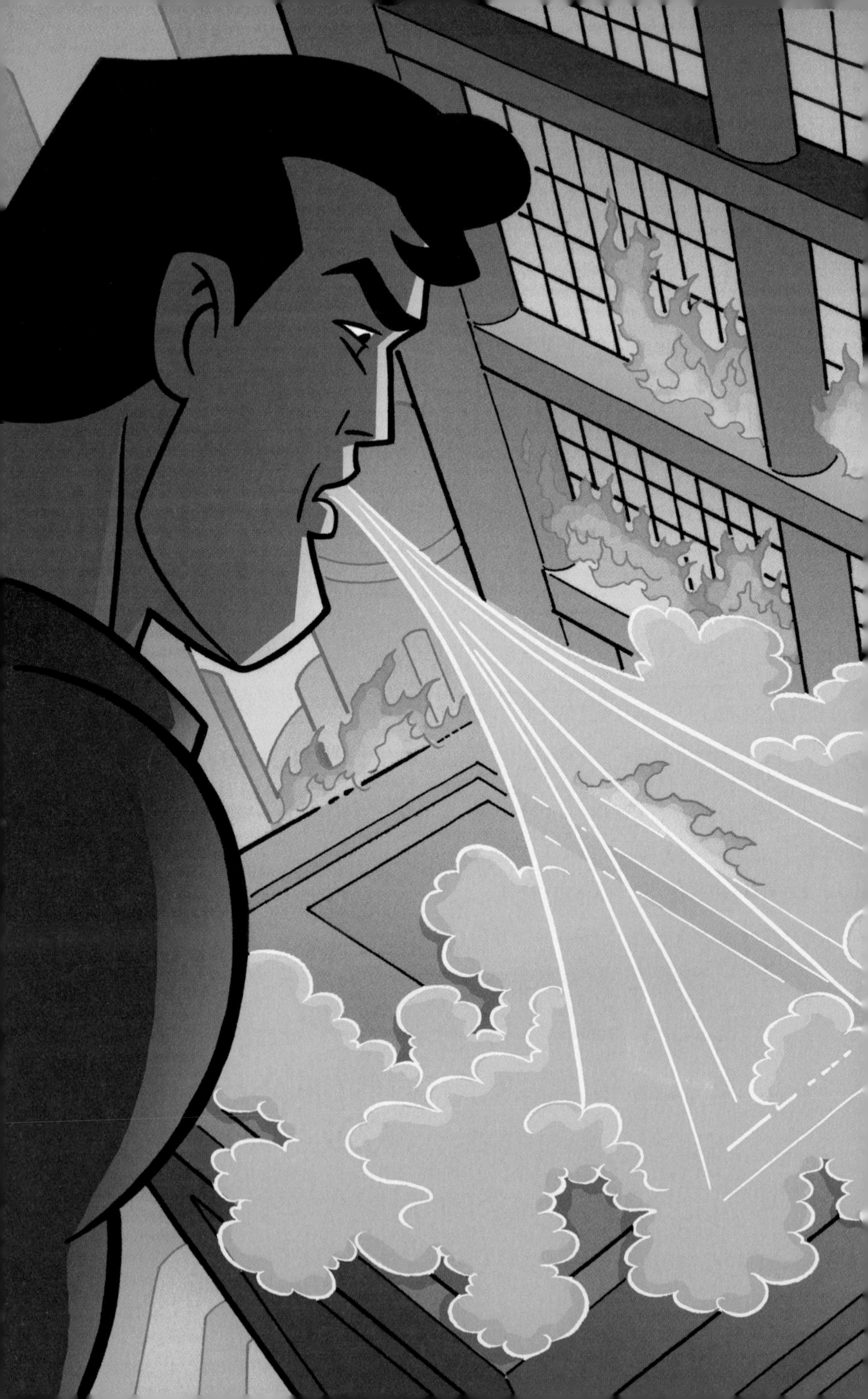

It worked like a charm. Suddenly, the flames in front of Superman got smaller. Then they disappeared completely. In their place, ice crystals formed on the outer edges of the charred building. Steam rose from the walls and the smoke began to clear. Superman had put out the fire as quickly as it had started.

As teams of firefighters arrived on the scene, Superman circled the building before flying off into the distance. His work was finished here, and he was in a hurry. After all, the sun would be setting soon, and Clark Kent still had a book to read.

*   *   *

This time Superman had found the perfect location. He didn't even change into his Clark Kent clothes. Instead, he perched himself on the rooftop of the Daily Planet.

Superman would finally have some quiet time. The street and its traffic were dozens of floors below him. The only sounds came from the nearby pigeons. There would be no more interruptions. It would just be him and his Kurt Vandelay novel.

Superman leaned back against the giant globe on the building's rooftop. He opened *Little Green Men* to the first page once again. He was reading about the little girl, and how the aliens were about to —

Superman looked up from his book. He saw what appeared to be a giant flying saucer, lowering itself to the street below.

"You've got to be kidding me," Superman said under his breath.

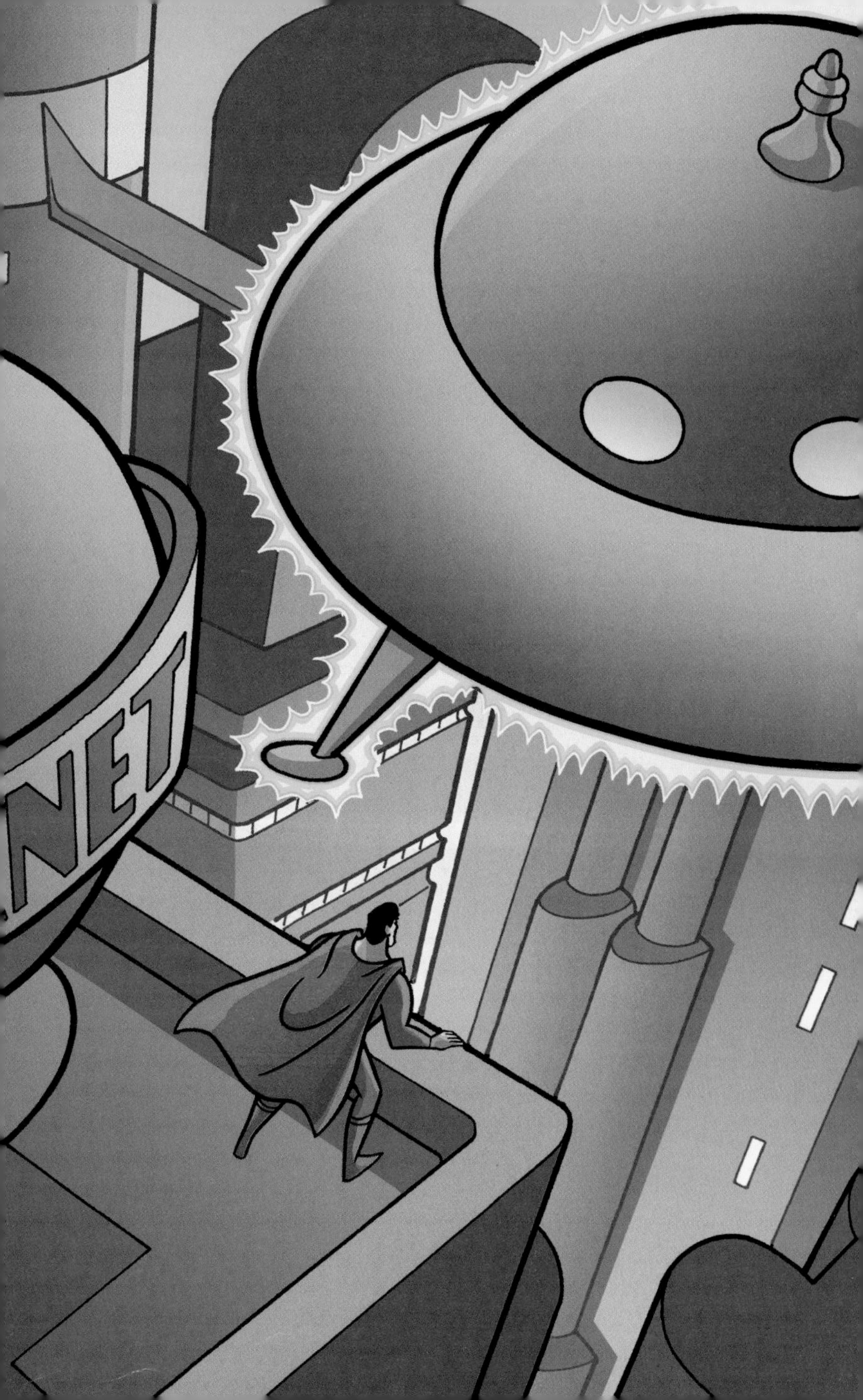
NET

CHAPTER 4

FLYING OFF THE PAGES

Superman gazed in disbelief over the ledge of the Daily Planet rooftop. A few stories below him hovered a flying saucer. The craft was bigger than a school bus and spun like a giant hubcap. But the really strange thing was, it looked almost exactly like the image on the cover of Superman's book.

As Superman watched, the space ship lowered itself in front of the glass doors of the building across the street. Superman knew the building well.

He passed by it almost every day on his way to work. It was the main branch of LexBank. As one of the largest banks in Metropolis, the building was famous. It held the money of many of the city's richest citizens.

Suddenly, a green ray shot out from the flying saucer. **BZZZT!** The bank's doors lit up in an eerie glow. People out for a stroll on the sidewalk ran away from the frightening spotlight. The green beam began to glow brighter and brighter. With the speed of lightning, the green light changed to bright white.

CRASH!! The bank's doors exploded off their hinges from the force of the strange laser beam. *There's no doubt about it*, Superman thought. *That spaceship is robbing the bank!*

Superman knew he had to act. He tucked his novel under his arm and leaped off the Daily Planet's rooftop.

The spaceship aimed its weapon above the doorway and fired again. BOOM!

Chunks of concrete and steel flew in all directions. Most of the civilians had fled to safety, but one elderly man had been knocked down in all the commotion. He was lying on the sidewalk near the bank's entrance, struggling to get to his feet. Suddenly, he heard a sound overhead. The old man looked up just in time to see a large chunk of the concrete wall heading straight for him. He raised his thin arms to shield himself.

The next thing he knew, the old man was sitting on a bench in the park. Superman was standing in front of him.

"You'll be safe here," Superman said.

"Oh," was all the old man could reply.

WHOOOOSH! A half-second later, Superman was back at the bank. He stared up at the hovering spacecraft.

"Enough of this," Superman said.

Rising into the air, Superman positioned himself in front of the green laser beam. Using his X-ray vision, Superman quickly scanned the ship. There was no one onboard. There wasn't a single living creature — not even an alien. The only thing he heard was a faint humming sound. Superman almost cracked a smile. His job had just become a lot easier.

Suddenly, the green beam turned from green to bright white. It filled the air with electricity.

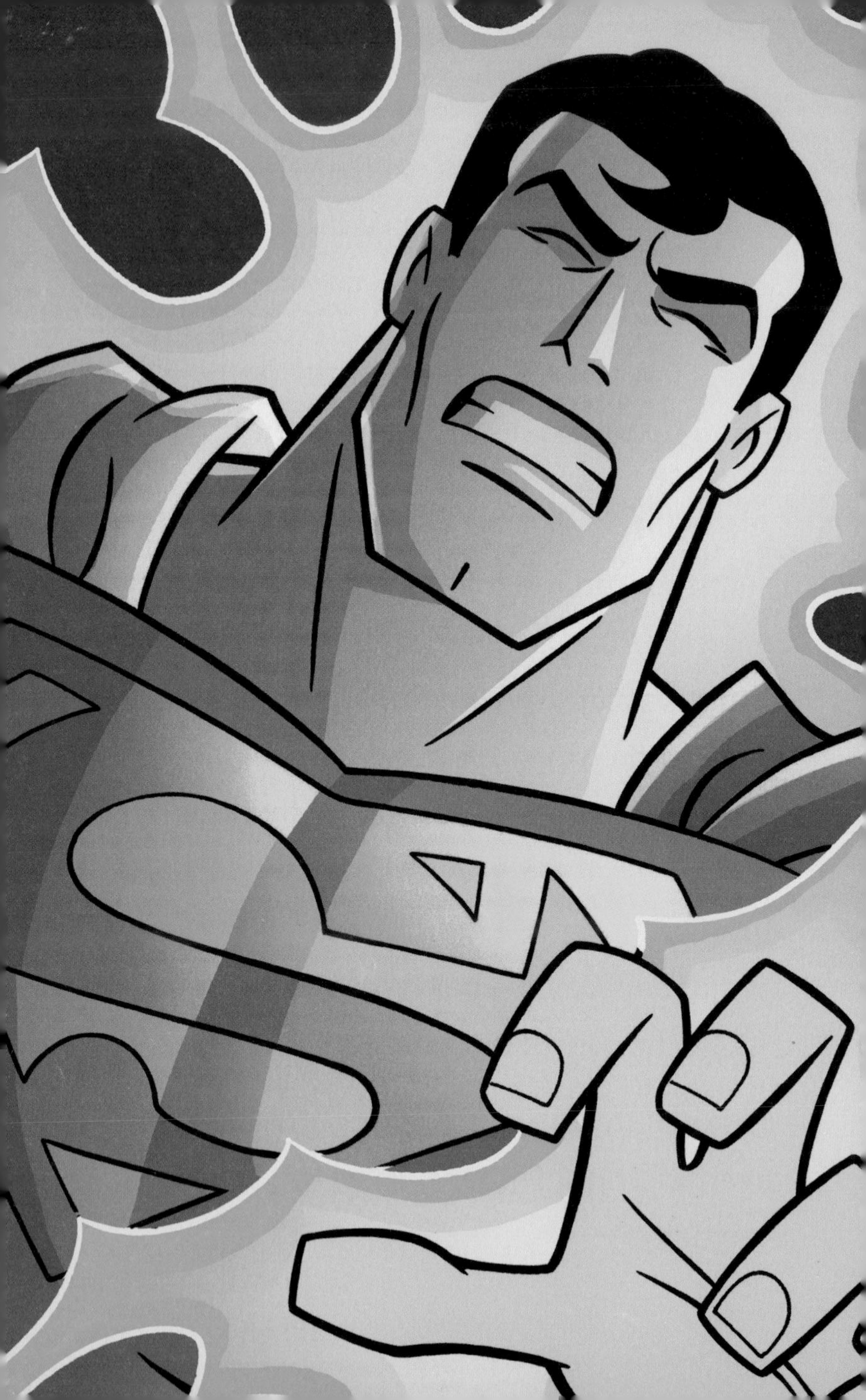

BZZT! Superman was struck by the intense lightning. It knocked him to the ground below. Shaking his head, Superman stood back up. Once again, he flew up into the light of the green beam.

BZZT! The laser fired again. This time, it only knocked Superman back a few feet. Superman hovered back to his position in front of the flying saucer for a third time.

BZZT! Once more the laser fired its lightning burst. And this time, Superman didn't move at all.

"Are you done yet?" Superman asked in an annoyed tone. The spaceship didn't answer. He didn't expect it to.

Superman flew closer to the saucer. He flexed his mighty muscles and drew back his right arm.

With all his super-strength, the Man of Steel delivered an uppercut punch to the bottom of the craft. **KA-POW!**

One punch was all that it took. The spaceship shot up into the air from the force of Superman's blow. Superman craned his head back to look at the ship as it sailed through the sky.

ZZZAPPPPPP! Red beams shot out of Superman's eyes. His heat vision struck the saucer's fuel storage compartment.

The entire flying saucer exploded into a cloud of green fire and smoke. The sight was almost as impressive as the Metropolis fireworks display that was held every year on the Fourth of July.

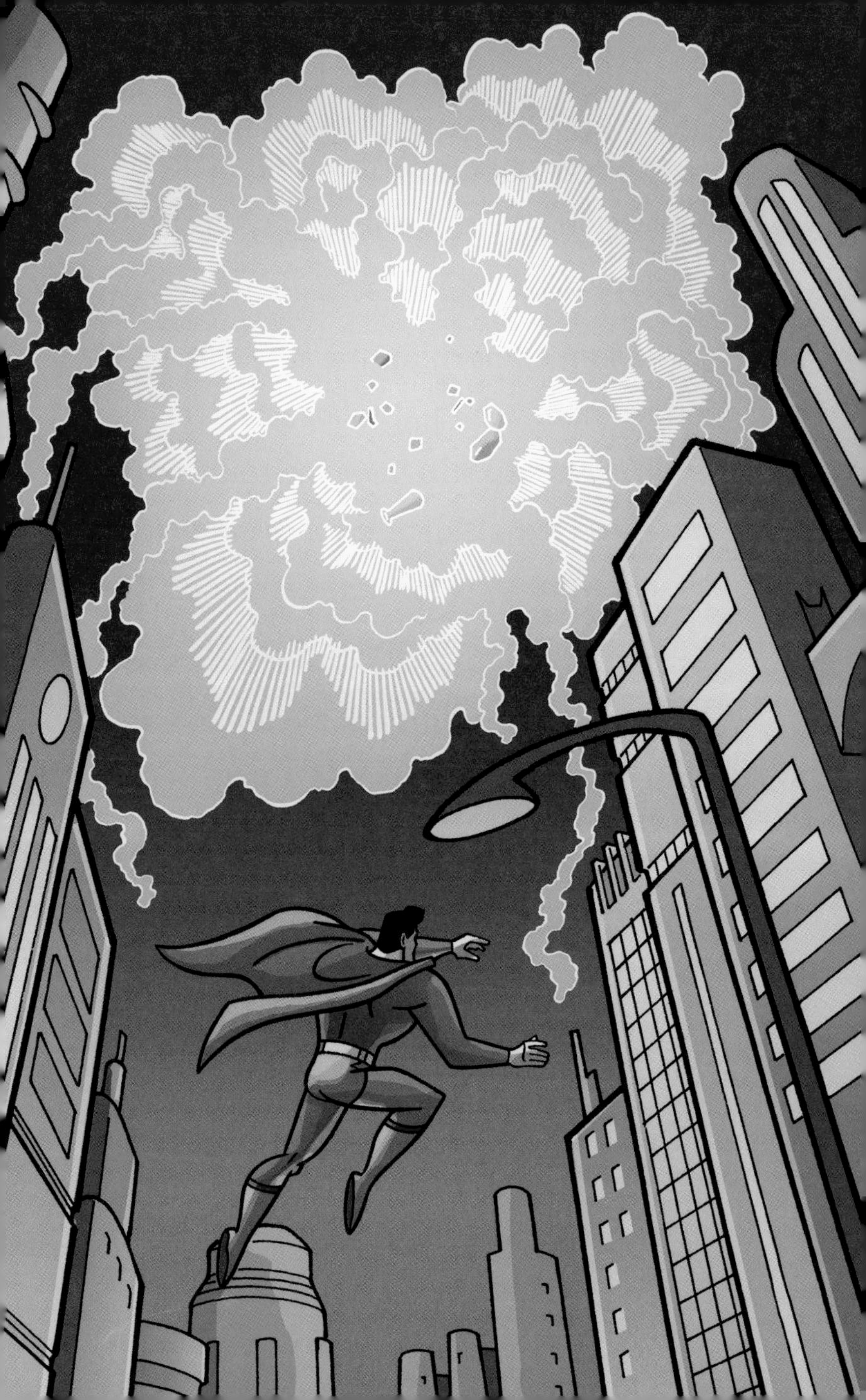

The saucer burst into thousands of tiny pieces. It safely burned away in the atmosphere.

As he landed back on the sidewalk, Superman knew the fight was not over. After all, he could still hear the faint sound he had detected inside the spaceship. He knew just what that humming meant. The noise was the result of radio waves.

That meant the ship was being operated by remote control.

Superman had a good idea of just who was controlling the joystick.

CHAPTER 5

WORDS TO LIVE BY

Superman focused his super-hearing. He concentrated on the low hum of the remote control. As he realized where the noise was coming from, Superman shook his head in surprise. The frequency seemed to start in the newsroom of the Daily Planet building. It was coming from the same floor where Clark Kent worked five days a week.

As a crowd began to form around the gaping hole that used to be the entrance to the bank, Superman shot off in a blur of blue and red.

Superman flew through the revolving door of the Daily Planet building and past the confused security guard. He zipped up the stairwell to his familiar office and stopped beside the elevators.

As he walked through the halls of the building, Superman used his X-ray vision to scan the floor. The entire building seemed to be completely empty. That is, until he spotted the supply closet near the restrooms. There was a small man huddled by the closet's window.

A second passed, and the little man felt a tap on his shoulder. He turned away from the window and nearly ran smack into the "S" symbol on Superman's chest. The man looked up. He dropped the remote control he was holding in his hands.

"Superman," he said quietly.

"I thought it would be you, Toyman," Superman said.

The little man hiding in the closet was none other than Winslow Schott Jr. He was also known as the Toyman, a genius inventor and criminal. Superman had stopped his many toy-related crimes time and time again. *He should know better by now,* Superman thought.

"You ruined my game," the little man said softly. He raised his masked face toward Superman.

As Toyman looked up, Superman couldn't tell if the villain was frightened or calm. The Toyman's strange mask hid his expression. Winslow's voice was almost always absent of emotion, as well. That made it difficult to predict what he would do next.

"You've been causing me a lot of trouble today," Superman said. "Let me guess — it was your flying saucer that buzzed too close to the construction site on Shuster Street."

The Toyman didn't answer. He just stared straight ahead at the Man of Steel.

"You almost killed an innocent construction worker," Superman said, looking for some kind of response.

Instead, the Toyman just slipped his hand into his pocket. It was like he was searching for something.

"You were responsible for the attack on S.T.A.R. Labs, too," Superman said. "What were you after? Fuel for your phony spaceship?"

Toyman pulled his hand out of his pocket. It was balled up in a fist.

It seemed like the little criminal was clutching something small within the palm of his hand.

"Why go through all this effort for a simple bank robbery, Toyman?" Superman asked.

Toyman lowered his head and looked at his hand. "Toys can be expensive," he said calmly.

The Toyman slowly raised his hand and opened it. "Would you like a piece of candy?" he asked. On his palm rested a bright green jawbreaker wrapped in clear plastic. The little round object looked just like ordinary candy, except for one thing. The jawbreaker was glowing.

Immediately, Superman felt weak. "Kryptonite!" he gasped.

Superman grunted. He felt the pain in his knees first. They buckled slightly, as if by reflex. He began to slouch over until he was kneeling on the ground.

Then the pain shot up through his chest and his head. The jawbreaker was made of a rock called kryptonite. Anyone from Krypton, like Superman, was powerless when near its lethal radiation. It was the only substance in the universe that could truly hurt the Man of Steel.

"Works rather fast, doesn't it?" said the Toyman. Superman was certain the Toyman was smiling beneath his mask now.

"I had my pockets specially lined with lead to block the stone's radiation," Toyman said. "What's wrong, Superman? I thought you'd like my surprise."

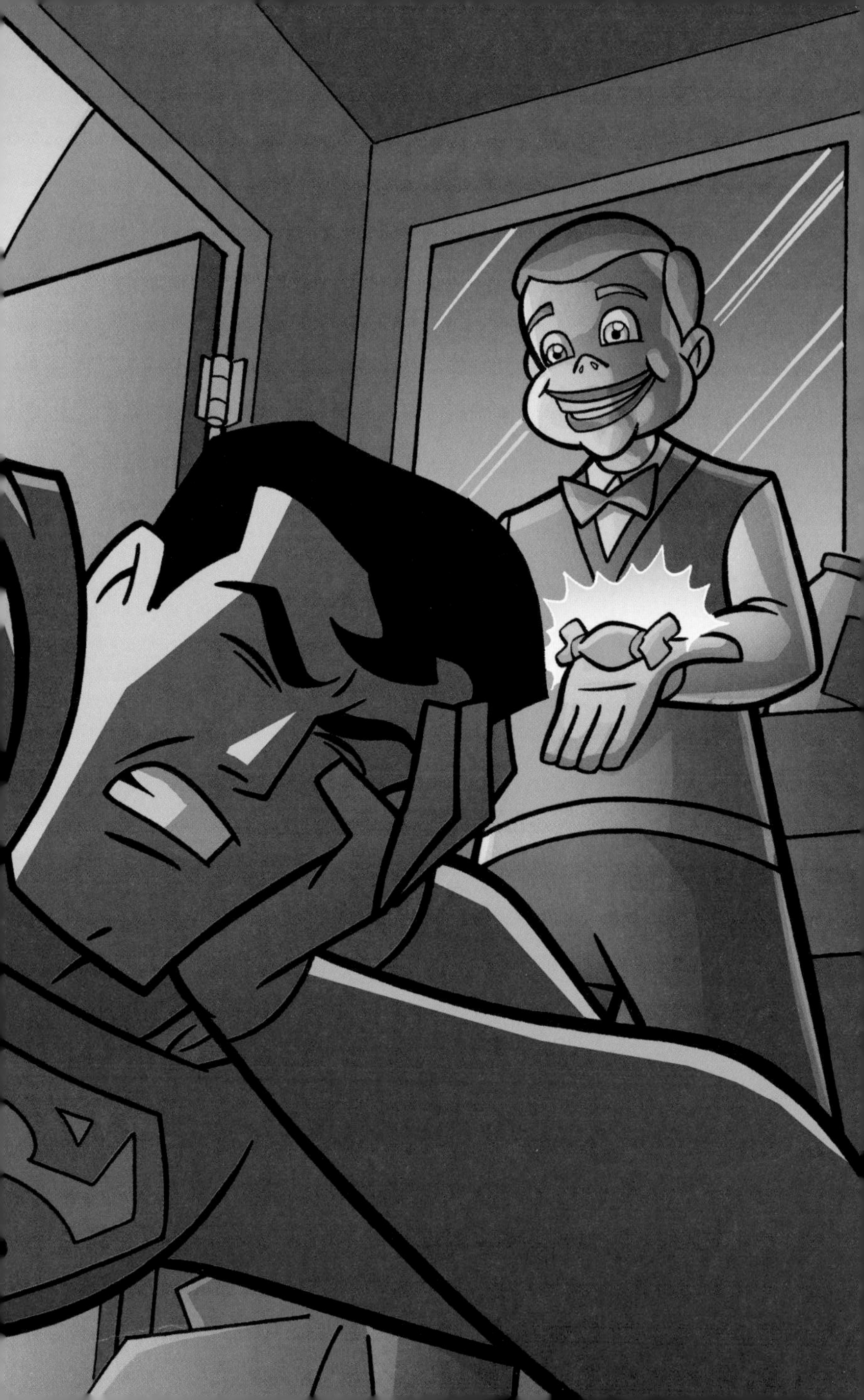

"But it looks like you're not too thrilled with it," he said. Toyman pushed the weakened super hero aside as if he were a child. Then he slowly walked past.

"Oh well. I guess I'll find somebody else to play with," he said.

Superman watched the Toyman stroll out into the hall and press the elevator button. The kryptonite in Schott's open hand continued to glow brightly. Superman had no choice but to watch him go. He felt as weak as a kitten.

Soon the elevator came. Toyman stepped inside the car. He waved to Superman as the doors closed.

As soon as the doors sealed themselves shut, Superman straightened himself. He felt his super-strength begin to return.

When the Toyman chose the Daily Planet as his lookout point, he didn't realize how old the building was. Many buildings had lead in them. In fact, the Daily Planet had lead-lined elevators walls! As long as the elevator doors were shut, radiation from the kryptonite wouldn't affect Superman at all.

With amazing speed, Superman pulled open the doors to the elevator shaft. He then flew into the shaft and grabbed the moving cables to Toyman's elevator car. Superman gave the thick cords a slight tug. **SNAP!** They quickly split in two, freeing the elevator car.

With the cables in hand, Superman flew toward the top of the elevator shaft. As he rose into the air, he carefully lifted the elevator car behind him.

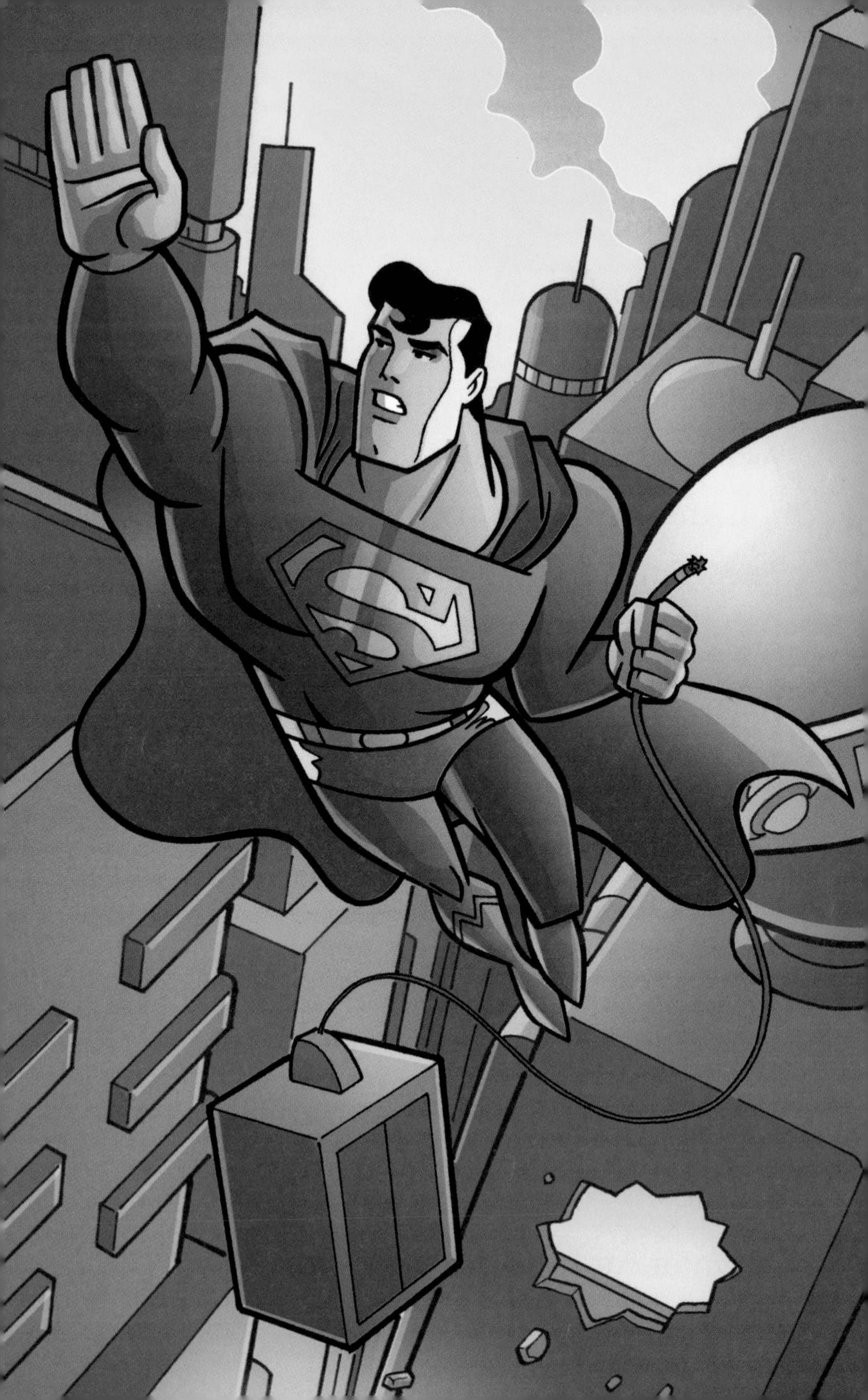

KRASSSHHH! Superman broke through the rooftop of the Daily Planet. Effortlessly, he lifted the elevator car up into the sky. With the criminal Toyman trapped securely inside, Superman carried the elevator car toward police headquarters.

As Superman flew in the direction of the setting sun, he chuckled to himself. He realized that he had spent his entire day off from work chasing little green men, instead of reading the book called *Little Green Men*.

*　　*　　*

Fifteen minutes later, the Man of Steel was back in front of the Daily Planet.

Just then, Superman looked around almost frantically. The Toyman was now in police custody, but Superman had another problem.

In all the commotion with the flying saucer, Superman had dropped his new book. He couldn't find it anywhere.

"You looking for this?" came a voice from behind him.

Superman turned around and looked into the eyes of the same elderly man he'd placed out of harm's way on a park bench earlier. The man was holding Superman's copy of *Little Green Men* out to him.

"Thanks," Superman said, taking the book. "I thought I'd lost that. I've been trying to read it all day, but haven't had any luck. The Toyman saw to that."

"Well, I'm glad that you took a break from your reading," said the old man. "I'll be the first to say that books are important, but so is real life experience."

"You'll learn a lot more out in the real world than you would from some silly sci-fi novel," the old man said.

Superman began to flip through his book to make sure it was okay. "Well, it's not just some silly sci-fi novel," he said. "It's written by . . . "

Superman paused. Someone had written on the title page of his book. It read, "To the Big Guy in Blue, Thanks for the save. All my best, Kurt Vandelay."

". . . Kurt Vandelay," Superman said under his breath. Now he realized who he was talking to. As he looked up, the old man was already gone.

Superman turned away and slowly flew off toward his apartment. For the second time today, he couldn't help but smile.

DAILY PLANET

WHO IS CLARK KENT?

Clark Kent's Kryptonian name is Kal-El. He was born on Krypton to Jor-El and Lara Lor-Van. Just before Krypton was destroyed, Kal-El was sent to Earth in one of Jor-El's spacecrafts. His parents decided they would send him to Earth so he would be safe. After landing in Smallville, Kansas, the young Kal-El was adopted by Jonathan and Martha, who gave him the name Clark. As he grew up, Clark took an interest in journalism. Since then, he has made a name for himself as one of the best reporters for the *Daily Planet*.

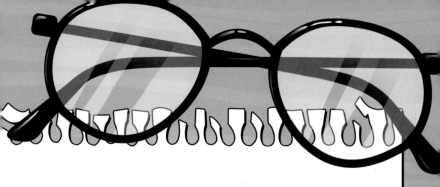

- The blanket that Kal-El's parents wrapped him in for the trip to Earth inspired Superman's costume. The blue and red cloth was sewn into a cape and tights by his adoptive mother, Martha.

- Clark Kent's favorite movie is To Kill a Mockingbird. Clark enjoys peanut butter and jelly sandwiches and football games. Clark's closest friends are Lois Lane, Jimmy Olsen, and Perry White — and all of them work at the Daily Planet with Clark.

- Clark Kent chose to become a reporter because the job would allow him to react quickly to threats against Metropolis. When bad news arrives, Clark makes a quick change into the Man of Steel and addresses the problem head-on! Afterward, Clark uses his first-hand experience to write a front-page story for the Daily Planet.

- Lana Lang was Clark Kent's first love, and she remains a close friend. She is one of the few people to know that Clark Kent is, in fact, the legendary Man of Steel. Years later, Clark met the reporter Lois Lane, and the two of them fell in love and married.

BIOGRAPHIES

Matthew K. Manning has more in common with Clark Kent than most people know. Like Superman, he was raised on a farm in the country and then moved to the big city to embark on a writing career. He has since written books or comics about Batman, Iron Man, Wolverine, the Legion of Super-Heroes, Spider-Man, the Incredible Hulk, and the Looney Tunes, including the recent hardcover history of Batman titled *The Batman Vault*. These days he lives in Brooklyn, New York, with his wife, Dorothy.

Erik Doescher is a freelance illustrator and video game designer based in Dallas, Texas. He attended the School of Visual Arts in New York City. Erik illustrated for a number of comic studios throughout the 1990s, and then moved to Texas to pursue videogame development and design. However, he has not completely given up on illustrating his favorite comic book characters.

Mike DeCarlo is a longtime contributor of comic art whose range extends from Batman and Iron Man to Bugs Bunny and Scooby-Doo. He resides in Connecticut with his wife and four children.

GLOSSARY

braced (BRAYSSD)—prepared yourself for a shock or the force of something hitting you

commotion (kuh-MOH-shuhn)—a lot of noisy, excited activity

eerie (EER-ee)—strange and frightening

faint (FAYNT)—soft and quiet

fascinated (FASS-uh-nate-id)—attracted and held the attention of

magnified (MAG-nuh-fyed)—made something appear larger so that it could be seen more easily

monotone (MON-uh-tohn)—if you speak in a monotone voice, the sound of your voice remains plain and dull

reflex (REE-fleks)—an automatic action that happens without a person's control or effort

surveyed (sur-VAYD)—looked at the whole scene

DISCUSSION QUESTIONS

1. Do you think aliens exist? Why or why not?

2. Clark Kent's favorite book is *Little Green Men* by Kurt Vandelay. What's your favorite book?

3. Toyman knows Superman's one weakness: kryptonite. What are some ways the Man of Steel could protect himself from kryptonite's deadly radiation?

WRITING PROMPTS

1. Superman gets to meet his favorite author in this book. If you could meet any famous person in the entire world, dead or alive, who would you choose? What kinds of questions would you ask? What would the two of you do together?

2. Imagine that aliens are invading your hometown. If you were a super hero, how would you defeat them? Write a short story about an alien attack.

3. Clark decides to stay home for his vacation. Where have you gone for vacation? Write about a family trip you've taken.

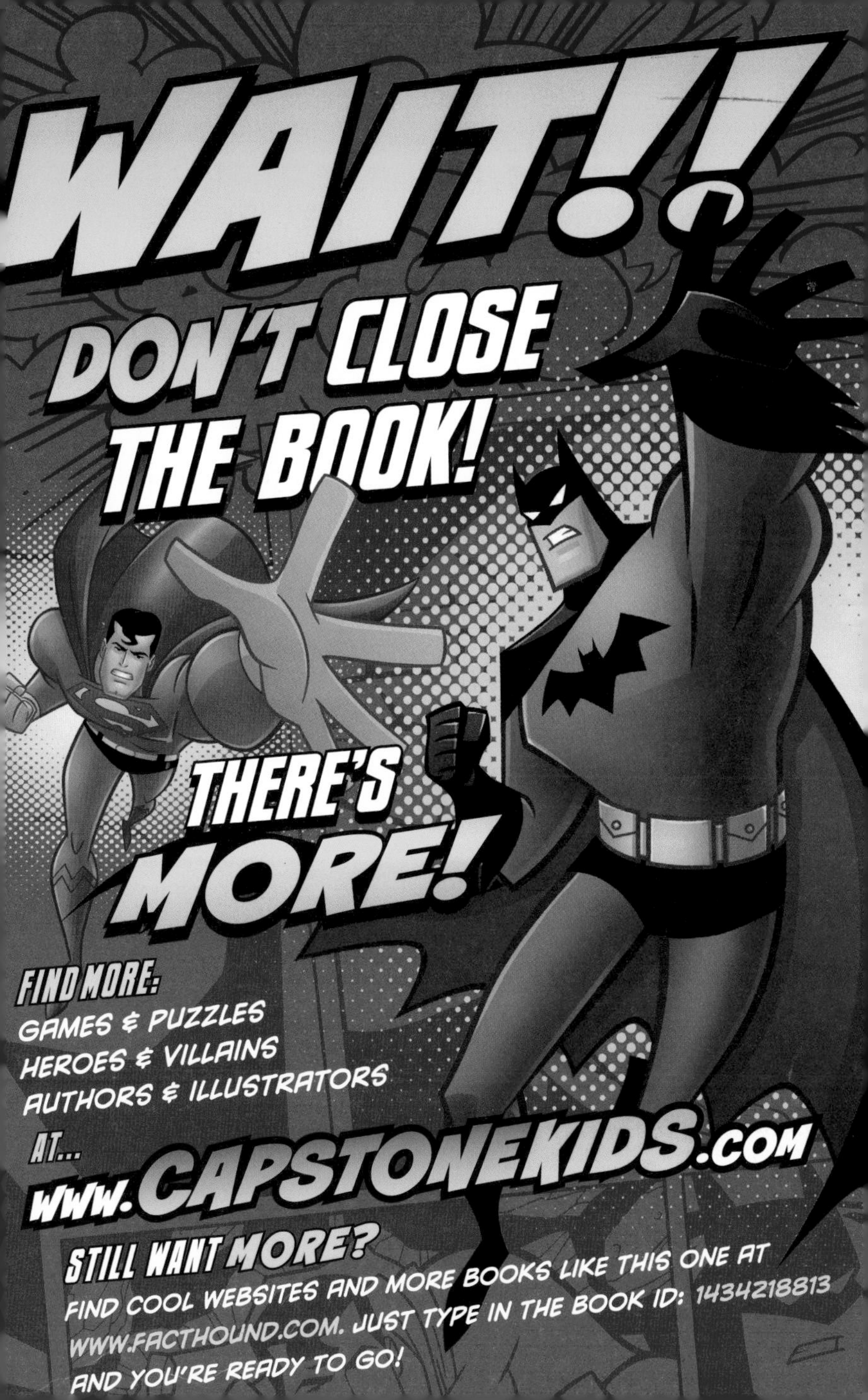
WAIT!!
DON'T CLOSE THE BOOK!
THERE'S MORE!
FIND MORE:
GAMES & PUZZLES
HEROES & VILLAINS
AUTHORS & ILLUSTRATORS
AT...
WWW.CAPSTONEKIDS.COM
STILL WANT MORE?
FIND COOL WEBSITES AND MORE BOOKS LIKE THIS ONE AT WWW.FACTHOUND.COM. JUST TYPE IN THE BOOK ID: 1434218813 AND YOU'RE READY TO GO!

MORE NEW SUPERMAN ADVENTURES!

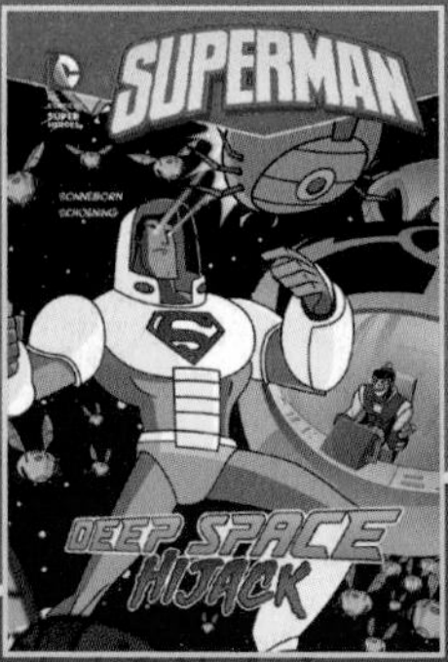
SUPERMAN
DEEP SPACE HIJACK

DEEP SPACE HIJACK

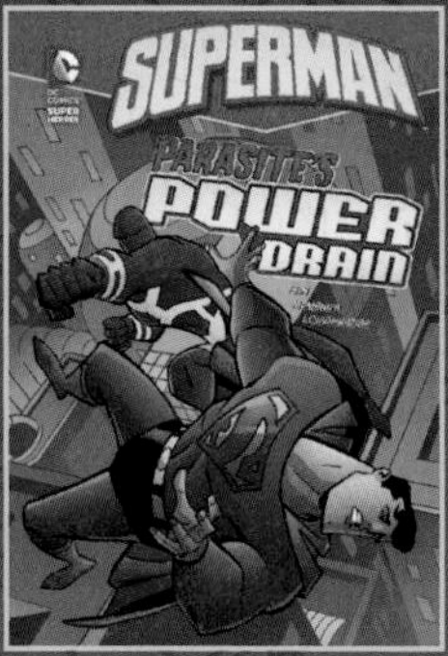
SUPERMAN
PARASITE'S POWER DRAIN

PARASITE'S POWER DRAIN

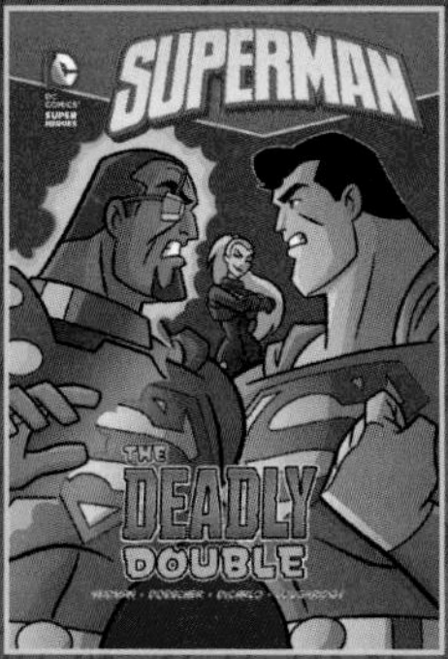
SUPERMAN
THE DEADLY DOUBLE

THE DEADLY DOUBLE

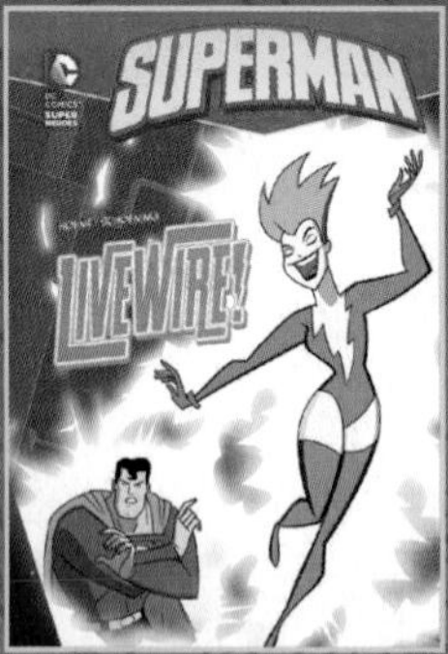
SUPERMAN
LIVEWIRE!

LIVEWIRE!

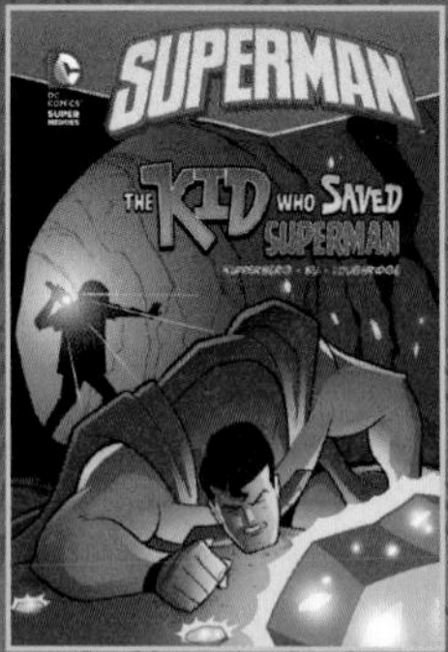
SUPERMAN
THE KID WHO SAVED SUPERMAN

THE KID WHO SAVED SUPERMAN